Dou

Written by April George

CONTENTS

Rigby

HOUGHTON MIFFLIN HARCOURT

How Animals Adapt to Lead Double Lives

Some creatures on Earth live double lives. These are animals that can live in water and on land.

Many of these creatures have special features or adaptations that help them lead their double lives. They have developed something special that makes them more suited to the different places they live.

Polar bears lead double lives. They hunt on the ice and in the ocean. Their cubs are born in snow caves.

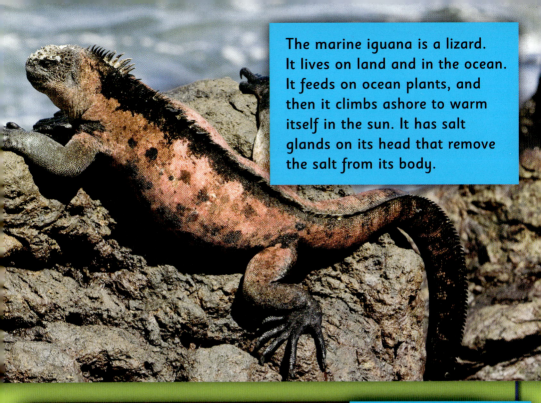

The marine iguana is a lizard. It lives on land and in the ocean. It feeds on ocean plants, and then it climbs ashore to warm itself in the sun. It has salt glands on its head that remove the salt from its body.

Frogs are amphibians that lead double lives because they can live on land and in the water.

How Frogs Adapt

Frogs are amphibians, and amphibians usually have larvae that hatch in water and breathe through gills. The larvae then turn into adults that have lungs and breathe air.

The skin of an amphibian is soft and damp. An amphibian will die if its skin dries out, so it needs to stay near water.

Tadpole

Did You Know?

The word amphibian comes from the Greek word *amphibios* meaning 'a being with a double life'.

Some frogs carry their tadpoles on their backs. They take them from pond to pond.

Life Cycle of a Frog

They become frogs.

Eggs are laid in the water.

Their tails grow shorter. They develop lungs to breathe air.

They grow back and front legs.

Larvae, called tadpoles, hatch from the eggs. The larvae breathe under water through gills.

How Mosquitoes Adapt

Some insects begin their lives in water. The mosquito lays its eggs in little 'rafts' on the water. The eggs hatch into larvae called wrigglers that come to the surface and hang upside down. They breathe through little tubes on their tails.

After about ten days, the wrigglers turn into pupae called tumblers. The tumblers float on the surface. The pupae breathe through two tubes called trumpets. If they are disturbed, they tumble below the surface.

Inside the tumbler, the adult mosquito grows. After a few days, the tumbler splits open, and an adult mosquito flies away. It will return to water to lay its eggs.

Mosquito egg raft

Mosquito laying eggs

mosquito eggs

Life Cycle of a Mosquito

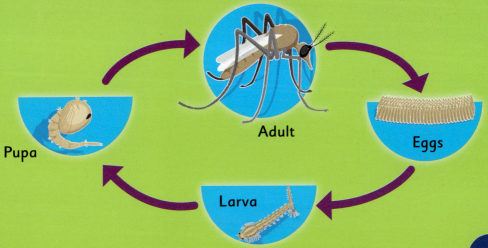

Adult

Eggs

Larva

Pupa

How Sea Turtles Adapt

Sea turtles are reptiles that spend most of their lives in water. They stay under water for a long time. They feed on jellyfish and small sea creatures. They breathe through lungs so they go to the surface to get air.

Sea turtles drink salt water. They have tear ducts behind their eyes that collect salt. The salt comes out of their eyes as tears.

Sea turtles lay their eggs on land. The female digs a hole in the sand for her eggs. She covers the eggs and returns to the water. When the eggs hatch, the babies run to the water to begin their watery lives.

These baby turtles have hatched and are running toward the safety of the water.

The pattern on the scales of each turtle's shell is different, just like our fingerprints!

Female turtle laying eggs in the sand

9

How Crocodiles Adapt

Crocodiles are reptiles that are well adapted to their double lives. They have nostrils on top of their snout that let them breathe while most of their body is hidden under the water. They have a throat flap that they can close to stop water from entering their windpipe. They have webbed toes and long, strong tails that help them swim.

Crocodiles need to go ashore to warm up in the sun, but beware of a sleeping crocodile. On land they can move fast, too!

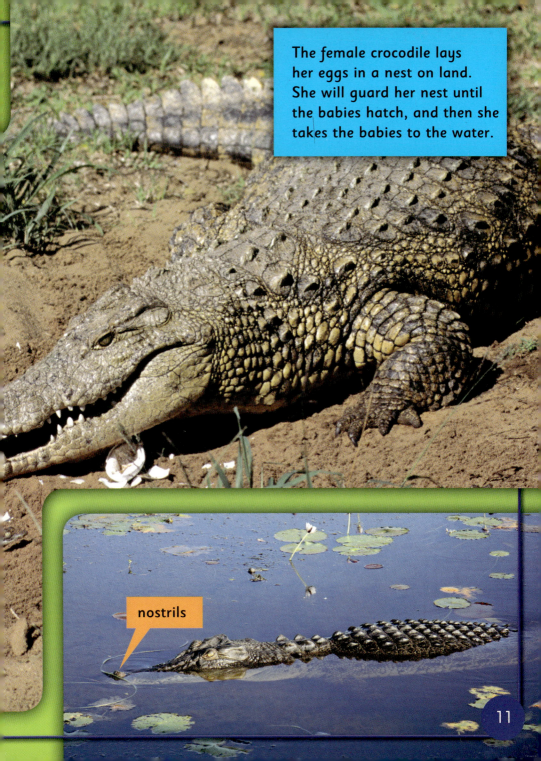

The female crocodile lays her eggs in a nest on land. She will guard her nest until the babies hatch, and then she takes the babies to the water.

nostrils

How Platypuses Adapt

Platypuses are mammals that live in streams in Australia. They are well adapted to their double lives. They dive and swim to catch their food, and they come to the surface to breathe. Like other mammals, the mothers feed their babies milk.

Platypuses have a bill like a duck and webbed feet for swimming. They can fold back the webs on their front feet so they can use their claws to walk on land and to dig. The females lay their eggs in burrows dug into the bank below the water.

bill

flat tail for swimming

webbed feet

How Hippos Adapt

Hippos are well adapted to their double lives, too. Hippos spend most of their day lazing in water. They use the water and mud to keep themselves cool. Hippos move easily in water and can stay under the water for up to 15 minutes. They often walk along on the bottom instead of swimming. Toward evening, they go ashore to eat grass. Hippos usually go back to the same pool at sunrise.

eyes on top of head

short strong tail used as a paddle when swimming

ears closed under water

four webbed toes on each foot for swimming

nostrils closed under water

Hippos live together in herds of about 10 to 20 animals. They communicate under water using clicks and whistles. Their babies are born under water and drink milk from their mothers under water, too.

Hippos may look half asleep in the water, but they are dangerous animals. They can fight well in water.

Hippos can run faster than a human on land.

How People Adapt Under Water

Many humans also spend a lot of time in water. Humans do not have special adaptations to help them live in water. They do not have webbed feet to help them swim. They do not have ears or throat flaps that they can close. However, people have invented things that help them swim faster and allow them to stay under water for a long time.

goggles

air tank

Scuba divers wear air tanks that allow them to breathe deep below the surface. The word 'scuba' is made up from the first letter of five different words: self-contained underwater breathing apparatus.

Index

flippers

Informational Explanations

Explanations explain how things work and why things happen.

How to Write an Informational Explanation

Step One

- Select a topic.
- Make a list of things you know about the topic.
- Brainstorm the questions you need to ask.

Step Two

- Research the thing you need to know.
- Use different resources for your research.

Internet

Library

Television documentaries

Experts

- Take notes or make copies of what you find.

Double Lives

How do animals adapt to lead double lives?
What animals live on land and in the water?
How do frogs adapt to live on land and in the water?
How do mosquitoes adapt?
How do sea turtles adapt?
How do crocodiles live on land and in water?
How do platypus adapt?
How do hippos adapt?
How do people adapt to being under water?

Step Three

- Sort through your notes. Organize related information under specific headings.

How Platypus Adapt:

- dive and swim to catch food
- come to the surface to breathe
- have a bill like a duck
- have webbed feet for swimming
- can fold back the webs on their front feet so they can use their claws to walk on land and to dig
- lay their eggs in burrows dug into the bank below the water

Step Four

- Use your notes to write your explanation.
- Introduce your topic.
- Add facts, details, and definitions from your research.
- Use quotations, examples, and vocabulary related to the topic.
- Use linking words and phrases, such as *another, for example, also,* and *because.*
- Provide a conclusion.

Your report may have:

a table of contents

an index

Some reports also have a glossary.

Guide Notes

Title: Double Lives

Stage: Advanced Fluency

Text Form: Informational Explanation

Approach: Guided Reading

Processes: Supporting Comprehension, Exploring Language, Processing Information

Writing Focus: Informational Explanation

SUPPORTING COMPREHENSION

- What do you think is the purpose of this book?
- How does the introduction text on page 2 explain the idea behind the topic?
- What inferences can you make about the special features or adaptations that animals have so they can lead a double life?
- How do you think droughts might impact amphibians?
- How do you think mosquito wrigglers would be affected by oil on the surface of the water?
- How might you find out the length of time turtles can stay under water?
- Why do you think crocodiles go ashore to warm up? What inferences can you make about this?
- What inferences can you make about how hippopotamuses can stay under water for 15 minutes?
- How do you think divers check on their gear before diving?
- What questions do you have after reading the text?
- What helped you understand the information?

EXPLORING LANGUAGE

Vocabulary
Clarify: adaptations, suited to, pupae, lungs, well adapted, mammals
Synonyms: Discuss synonyms for *damp*, *close*, *invented*
Antonyms: Discuss antonyms for *soft*, *begin*, *lazing*